W9-AMC-067

THE FLYING SHIP

THE FLYING SHIP

RETOLD BY ANDREW LANG

ILLUSTRATED BY DENNIS McDERMOTT

MORROW JUNIOR BOOKS
NEW YORK

Watercolors with colored pencils were used for the full-color illustrations.
The text type is 16-point Bembo.

Printed in the United States of America.
1 2 3 4 5 6 7 8 9 10

Library of Congress Cataloging-in-Publication Data
Lang, Andrew, 1844–1912. The flying ship/Andrew Lang; illustrated by Dennis McDermott. p. cm.
Summary: With the help of some extraordinary comrades that he meets on the way, a Simpleton
fulfills the King's outlandish requests and wins the hand of the Princess.
ISBN 0-688-11404-0 (trade)—ISBN 0-688-11405-9 (library)
[1. Fairy tales. 2. Folklore—Russia.] I. McDermott, Dennis, ill. II. Title.
PZ8.1.L25F1 1995 398.2'094702—dc20 94-42963 CIP AC

For Hayley and Devon

Once upon a time, there lived an old couple who had three sons; the two elder were clever, but the third was a regular dunce. The clever sons were very fond of their mother, gave her good clothes, and always spoke pleasantly to her; but the youngest was always getting in her way, and she had no patience with him.

Now, one day it was announced in the village that the King had issued a decree, offering his daughter, the Princess, in marriage to whoever should build a ship that could fly. Immediately the two elder brothers determined to try their luck and asked their parents' blessing. So the old mother smartened up their clothes and gave them a store of provisions for their journey. When they had gone, the poor Simpleton began to tease his mother to smarten him up and let him start off.

"What would become of a dolt like you?" she answered. "Why, you would be eaten up by wolves."

But the foolish youth kept repeating, "I will go, I will go, I will go!"

Seeing that she could do nothing with him, the mother gave him a crust of bread and a bottle of water, and took no further heed of him.

So the Simpleton set off on his way. When he had gone a short distance, he met a little old man. They greeted each other, and the little man asked him where he was going.

"I am off to the King's court," he answered. "He has promised to give his daughter to whoever can make a flying ship."

"And can you make such a ship?"

"Not I."

"Then why in the world are you going?"

"Can't tell," replied the Simpleton.

"Well, if that is the case," said the little man, "sit down beside me; we can rest for a little and have something to eat. Give me what you have got in your satchel."

Now, the poor Simpleton was ashamed to show what was in it. However, he thought it best not to make a fuss, so he opened the satchel and could scarcely believe his own eyes, for instead of the hard crust, he saw two beautiful fresh rolls and some cold meat. He shared them with the little man, who licked his lips and said:

"Now, go into that wood and stop in front of the first tree, bow three times, and then strike the tree with your ax, fall on your knees on the ground, with your face on the earth, and remain there till you are raised up. You will then find a ship at your side; step into it and fly to the King's palace. If you meet anyone on the road, take him with you."

The Simpleton thanked the little man very kindly, bade him farewell, and went into the road. When he got to the first tree, he stopped in front of it, did everything just as he had been told, and, kneeling on the ground with his face to the earth, fell asleep. After a little time he was roused; he awoke and, rubbing his eyes, saw a ready-made ship at his side and at once got into it.

And the ship rose and rose, and in another minute was flying through the air when the Simpleton, who was on the lookout, cast his eyes down to the earth and saw a man beneath him on the road, who was kneeling with his ear upon the damp ground.

"Hello!" he called out. "What are you doing down there?"

"I am listening to what is going on in the world," replied the man.

"Come with me in my ship," said the Simpleton.

So the man was only too glad and got in beside him; and the ship flew, and flew, and flew through the air, till again from his lookout the Simpleton saw a man on the road below, who was hopping on one leg while his other leg was tied up behind his ear. So he hailed him, calling out:

"Hello! What are you doing, hopping on one leg?"

"I can't help it," replied the man. "I walk so fast that unless I tie up one leg, I should be at the end of the earth in a bound."

“Come with us on my ship,” he answered, and the man made no objections, but joined them. And the ship flew on, and on, and on, till suddenly the Simpleton, looking down on the road below, beheld a man aiming with a gun into the distance.

“Hello!” he shouted to him. “What are you aiming at? As far as eye can see, there is no bird in sight.”

“What would be the good of my taking a near shot?” replied the man. “I can hit beast or bird at a hundred miles’ distance. That is the kind of shot I enjoy.”

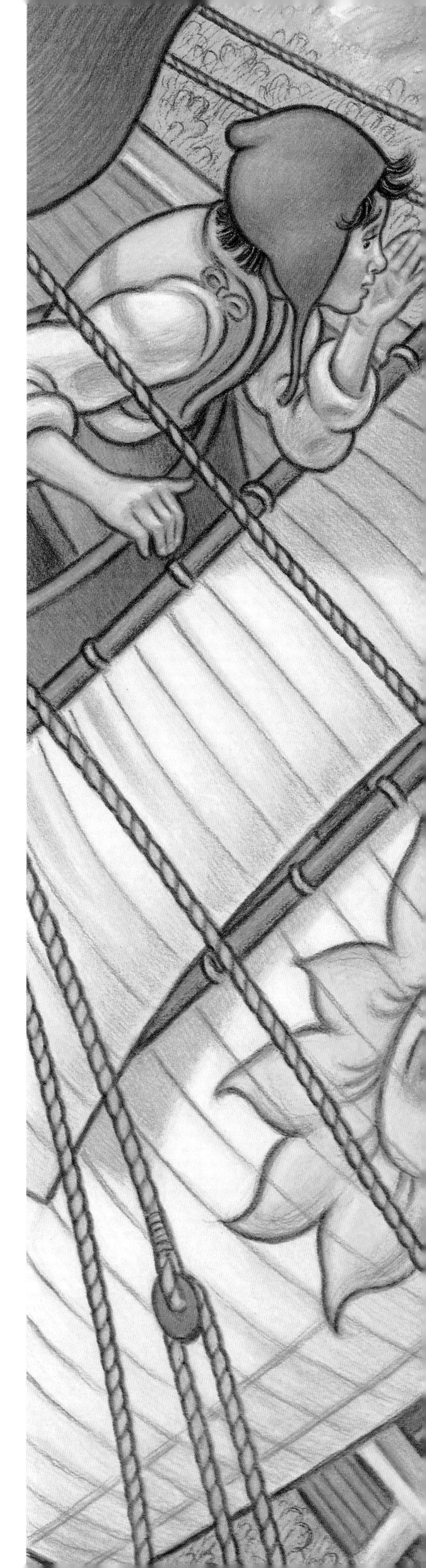

"Come into the ship with us," answered the Simpleton, and the man was only too glad to join them, and he got in. And the ship flew on, farther and farther, till again the Simpleton from his lookout saw a man on the road below, carrying on his back a basket full of bread. And he waved to him, calling out:

"Hello! Where are you going?"

"To fetch bread for my breakfast."

"Bread? Why, you have got a whole basketload of it on your back."

"That's nothing," answered the man. "I should finish that in one mouthful."

"Come along with us in my ship, then."

And so the hungry man joined the party. And the ship mounted again into the air and flew up and onward till the Simpleton from his lookout saw a man walking by the shore of a great lake, evidently looking for something.

"Hello!" he cried to him. "What are you seeking?"

"I want water to drink—I'm so thirsty," replied the man.

"Well, there's a whole lake in front of you. Why don't you drink some of that?"

"Do you call that enough?" answered the other. "Why, I should drink it up in one gulp."

"Well, come with us in the ship."

And so the man with the mighty thirst was added to the company, and the ship flew farther, and even farther, till again the Simpleton looked out, and this time he saw a man dragging a bundle of wood, walking through the forest beneath them.

"Hello!" he shouted to him. "Why are you carrying wood through a forest?"

"This is not common wood," answered the other.

"What sort of wood is it, then?" asked the Simpleton.

"If you throw it upon the ground," said the man, "it will be changed into an army of soldiers."

"Come into the ship with us, then."

And so he too joined them. And away the ship flew, on, and on, and on, and once more the Simpleton looked out, and this time he saw a man carrying straw upon his back.

"Hello! Where are you carrying that straw?"

"To the village," said the man.

"Do you mean to say there is no straw in the village?"

"Ah! But this is quite a peculiar straw. If you strew it about even in the hottest summer, the air at once becomes cold, and snow falls, and the people freeze."

Then the Simpleton asked him also to join them.

At last the ship, with its strange crew, arrived at the King's court. The King was having his dinner, but he at once dispatched one of his courtiers to find out what the huge, strange new bird could be that had come flying through the air. The courtier peeped into the ship and, seeing what it was, instantly went back to the King and told him that it was a flying ship, and that it was manned by a few peasants.

Then the King remembered his royal oath, but he made up his mind

that he would never consent to let the Princess marry a poor peasant. So he thought and thought, and then said to himself:

"I will give him some impossible tasks to perform; that will be the best way of getting rid of him." And he there and then decided to dispatch one of his courtiers to the Simpleton with the command that he was to fetch the King the healing water from the world's end before the King had finished his dinner.

But while the King was still instructing the courtier exactly what he was to say, the first man of the ship's company, the one with the miraculous power of hearing, had overheard the King's words and hastily reported them to the poor Simpleton.

"Alas, alas!" he cried. "What am I to do now? It would take me quite a year, possibly my whole life, to find the water."

"Never fear," said his fleet-footed comrade. "I will fetch what the King wants."

Just then the courtier arrived, bearing the King's command.

"Tell His Majesty," said the Simpleton, "that his orders shall be obeyed." And the swift runner unbound the foot that was strung up behind his ear and started off, and in less than no time had reached the world's end and drawn the healing water from the well.

"Dear me," he thought to himself, "that's rather tiring! I'll just rest for a few minutes. It will be some little time yet before the King gets to dessert." So he threw himself down on the grass, and as the sun was very dazzling, he closed his eyes and in a few minutes had fallen sound asleep.

In the meantime, all the ship's crew were anxiously awaiting him. The King's dinner would soon be finished, and their comrade had not yet returned. So the man with the marvelous quick hearing lay down and, putting his ear to the ground, listened.

"That's a nice sort of fellow!" he suddenly exclaimed. "He's lying on the ground, snoring hard!"

At this, the marksman seized his gun, took aim, and fired in the direction of the world's end in order to awaken the sluggard. And a moment later the swift runner reappeared and, stepping on board the ship, handed the healing water to the Simpleton. So while the King was still sitting at the table finishing his dinner, news was brought to him that his orders had been obeyed to the letter.

What was to be done now? The King determined to think of a still more impossible task. So he told another courtier to go to the Simpleton with the command that he and his comrades were instantly to eat up twelve oxen and twelve tons of bread. Once more, the sharp-eared comrade overheard the King's words while he was still talking to the courtier and reported them to the Simpleton.

"Alas, alas!" he sighed. "What in the world shall I do? Why, it would take us a year, possibly our whole lives, to eat up twelve oxen and twelve tons of bread."

"Never fear," said the hungry man. "It will scarcely be enough for me. I'm so hungry."

So when the courtier arrived with the royal message, he was told to take back word to the King that his orders would be obeyed. Then twelve roasted oxen and twelve tons of bread were brought alongside the ship, and at one sitting the hungry man had devoured it all.

"I call that a small meal," he said. "I wish they'd brought me some more."

Next, the King ordered that forty casks of water, containing forty gallons each, were to be drunk up on the spot by the Simpleton and his party. When these words were overheard by the sharp-eared comrade and repeated to the Simpleton, he was in despair.

"Alas, alas!" he exclaimed. "What is to be done? It would take us a year, possibly our whole lives, to drink so much."

"Never fear," said his thirsty comrade. "I'll drink it all up at a gulp, see if I don't." And sure enough, when the forty casks of water containing forty gallons each were brought alongside the ship, they disappeared down the thirsty comrade's throat in no time. And when they were empty, he remarked:

"Why, I'm still thirsty. I should have been glad of two more casks."

Then the King took counsel with himself and sent an order to the Simpleton that he was to have a bath in a bathroom at the royal palace, and after that the betrothal should take place. Now, the bathroom was built of iron, and the King gave orders that it was to be heated to such a pitch that it would suffocate the Simpleton.

And so when the poor silly youth entered the room, he discovered that the iron walls were red-hot. But, fortunately, his comrade with the straw on his back had entered behind him, and when the door was shut upon them, he scattered the straw about, and suddenly the red-hot walls cooled down, and it became so very cold that the Simpleton could scarcely bear to take a bath, and all the water in the room froze.

So the Simpleton climbed on the stove and, wrapping himself up in the bath blankets, lay there the whole night. And in the morning when they opened the door, there he lay sound and safe, singing cheerfully to himself.

Now, when this strange tale was told to the King, he became quite sad, not knowing what he should do to get rid of so undesirable a son-in-law, when suddenly a brilliant idea occurred to him.

"Tell the rascal to raise me an army, now, at this instant!" he exclaimed to one of his courtiers. "Inform him at once of this, my royal will." And to himself he added, "I think I shall do for him this time."

As on former occasions, the quick-eared comrade had overheard the King's command and repeated it to the Simpleton.

"Alas, alas!" he groaned. "Now I am quite done for."

"Not at all," replied one of his comrades (the one who had dragged the bundle of wood through the forest). "Have you quite forgotten me?"

In the meantime, the courtier, who had run all the way from the palace, reached the ship panting and breathless, and delivered the King's message.

"Good!" remarked the Simpleton. "I will raise an army for the King." And he drew himself up. "But if, after that, the King refuses to accept

me as his son-in-law, I will wage war against him and carry the Princess off by force."

During the night, the Simpleton and his comrade went together into a big field, not forgetting to take the bundle of wood with them, which the man spread out in all directions. And in a moment a mighty army stood upon the spot, regiment on regiment of foot and horse soldiers. The bugles sounded and the drums beat, the chargers neighed, and their riders put their lances in their holders and the soldiers presented arms.

THE FLYING SHIP

In the morning when the King awoke, he was startled by these warlike sounds: the bugles and the drums, and the clatter of the horses, and the shouts of the soldiers. And stepping to the window, he saw the lances gleam in the sunlight and the armor and weapons glitter. And the proud monarch said to himself, "I am powerless in comparison with this man." So he sent him royal robes and costly jewels, and commanded him to come to the palace to be married to the Princess. And his son-in-law put on the royal robes, and he looked so grand and stately that it was impossible to recognize the poor Simpleton, so changed was he; and the Princess fell in love with him as soon as ever she saw him.

Never before had so grand a wedding been seen, and there was so much food and drink that even the hungry and the thirsty comrades had enough to eat and drink.